KILLER WHALE EYES

Written and Illustrated by

SONDRA SIMONE SEGUNDO

SEALASKA HERITAGE INSTITUTE

Juneau

SEALASKA HERITAGE INSTITUTE
One Sealaska Plaza, Suite 301
Juneau, Alaska 99801
907.463.4844 • 907.586.9293 (f)
www.sealaskaheritage.org • www.jineit.com

Library of Congress Control Number: 2013957054
ISBN 978–0–9853129–5–4

Killer Whale Eyes / written and illustrated by Sondra Simone Segundo.

Cover: *Killer Whale Eyes* by Sondra Simone Segundo.

Song: *I am a Child of the Ocean* performed by Sondra Simone Segundo.
Recorded at Front Burner Studio in Seattle, Washington.

Design and composition by Kathy Dye.

This book was funded in part by grants from Potlatch Fund, Evergreen
Longhouse, and Sealaska Heritage Institute.

For my elders, Uncle Miijuu, Auntie Viola, and Auntie Louise, who have recently joined the spirit world. They were the last of our fluent speakers who spoke our dialect since birth. Haw'aa/Thank you my dear uncle and sweet aunties for your love and wisdom. Your legacy lives on.

INTRODUCTION

I created this whale tale from Haida stories that were passed down over the years. We believe that our spirits become one with the ravens, eagles, wolves, bears, salmon, seals, killer whales, frogs, and other beautiful life that surrounds our land. We treat these lives with honor and respect.

Many Native people call orcas killer whales because they are natural hunters and protectors. They are known not to harm people. On my tribal lands, there have been many true instances of killer whales helping us. One example is of them guiding boats back to shore during a storm.

Haida words used in *Killer Whale Eyes* include:

- grandfather—chanáa
- dear one—dagwáang
- grandmother—náanaa
- whale—kún
- girl—jáadaas

Way back in time—about 423 years to be exact—in a Haida village by the sea, a little girl was born with eyes like no other.

Her eyes were unique and as blue as the ocean deep. When her beloved Haida people looked into these deep blue eyes, a feeling of quiet wonder came over them, like when you look out to sea on a warm summer day and know that the world is magic.

The little girl belonged to
the Killer Whale House—
one of many crest houses
and clans in the village—
and she loved to play in the
water. As a young girl, her
favorite playtime activity
was swimming with the sea
otters. She liked to hold the
tiny babies in her hands.

She was so gentle and kind that the mama otters trusted her with their little ones. They, too, felt a quiet wonder when they looked into her eyes. During these alone times with her friends of the sea, she sang her song. It was a song that the people came to know and love, for it echoed the wondrous sounds of the ocean.

As she grew into a young woman, her chanáa (grandpa) taught her how to carve. She showed amazing talent in this skill.

Together, they worked on a
very special canoe.

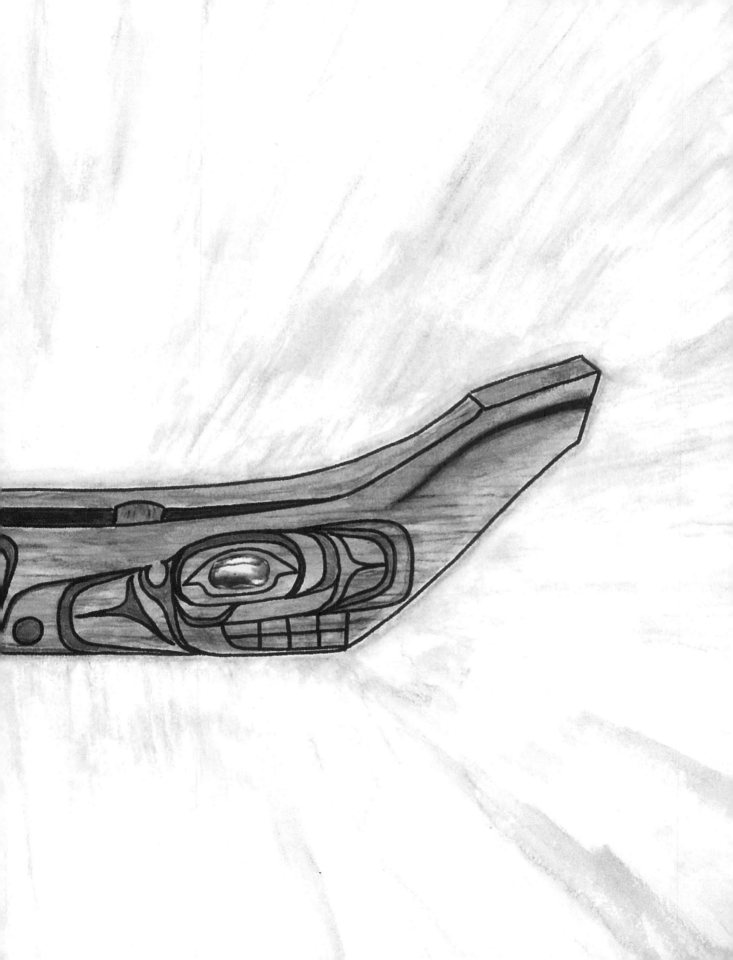

When the canoe was finished, they prepared to celebrate.

Everyone was so busy, they did not notice that their dagwáang (dear one) was not helping.

She was down by the water's edge, gazing at the canoe. Gradually, a warm feeling began to build inside her chest. She closed her eyes and imagined herself far from land, paddling strong and fast.

She opened her eyes and to her great
surprise, she wasn't just imagining it!
The village was ready to celebrate. They
called out to their dagwáang—no answer.
The canoe and the girl were gone.

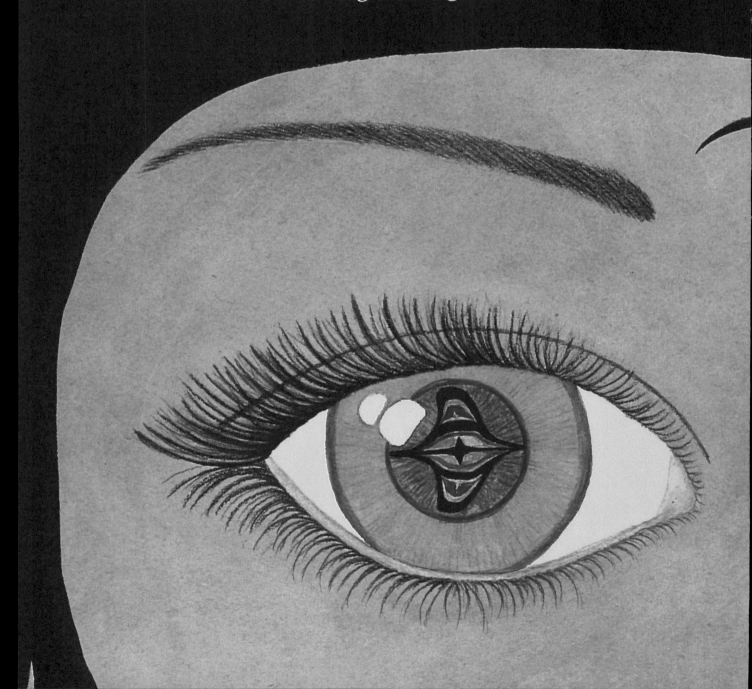

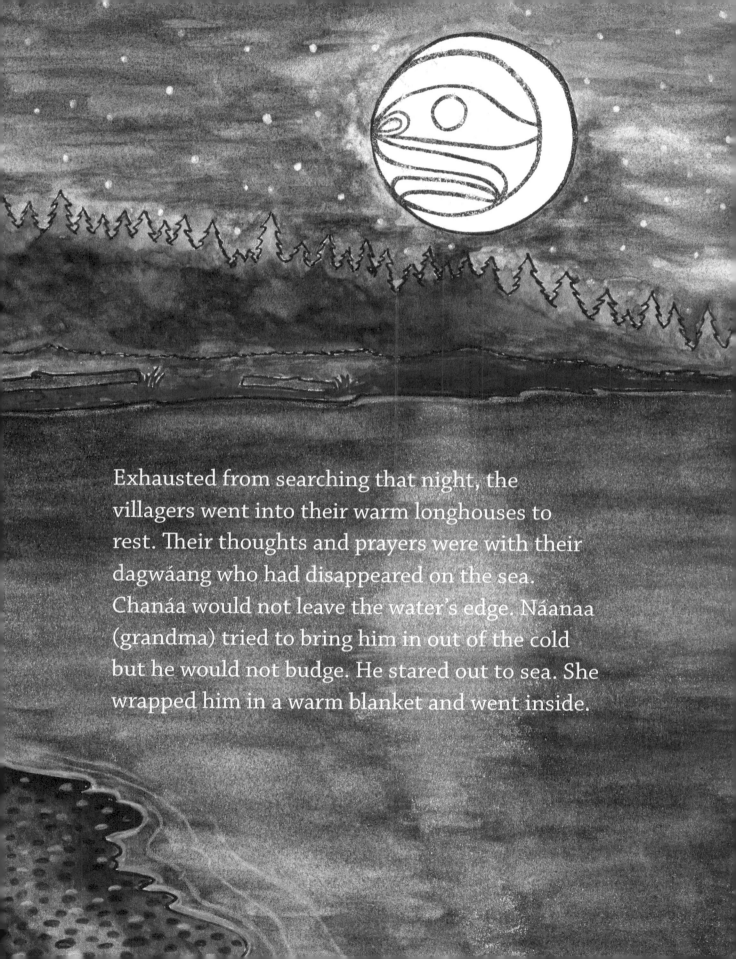

Exhausted from searching that night, the
villagers went into their warm longhouses to
rest. Their thoughts and prayers were with their
dagwáang who had disappeared on the sea.
Chanáa would not leave the water's edge. Náanaa
(grandma) tried to bring him in out of the cold
but he would not budge. He stared out to sea. She
wrapped him in a warm blanket and went inside.

As the sun rose the next morning, chanáa was still waiting. His eyes were tired, and his body was chilled from the cool sea air. Suddenly, he saw the canoe! It was floating in with the tide! How happy he was! But when the canoe reached the shore, chanáa could see only her clothes and the paddle. She was not there.

Time passed as it always does—about four seasons to be exact—yet the hearts of the people still ached. The people of the Killer Whale House decided to have a ceremony in honor of their dagwáang. Since her disappearance, the canoe had never been used. The people knew this was not right, so the canoe was once again carried to shore and launched. The people plunged their paddles into the water and were on their way. They paddled to the beat of chanáa's drumming and sang their dagwáang's special song.

DAGWÁANG'S SPECIAL SONG

"Síigaay gid uu díi íijang.

I am a child of the ocean.

Díi hal kyáagaangs Hl gudánggang.

I hear her calling to me.

Sg_áanaay gyaa Sg alangáay eehl díig hal kyáagaanggang.

Through the song of my relative killer whale

Díi hal kyáagaangs Hl gudánggang.

I hear her calling to me"

Listen to "I am a Child of the Ocean" by scanning the QR code with your smart phone, typing the url http://bit.ly/1gcWGGB into your browser, or using the CD that comes with the book sold through Sealaska Heritage Institute.

Just then, a pod of killer whales surfaced. They, too, sang a song. It calmed the people. Slowly, the canoe drifted to a stop. The people and the whales had no fear of one another. They shared a peaceful love and respect.

Chanáa looked into the eyes of one of the whales and saw that it was crying. He told the whale to come closer. They looked into each other's eyes and he understood that these were not tears of sadness, but of joy! In that moment, he realized that this whale had his granddaughter's beautiful eyes and spirit! It was their dagwáang! Oh, how their hearts were full of love and amazement as Kún Jáadaas (Whale Girl) greeted the people. How they had missed one another.

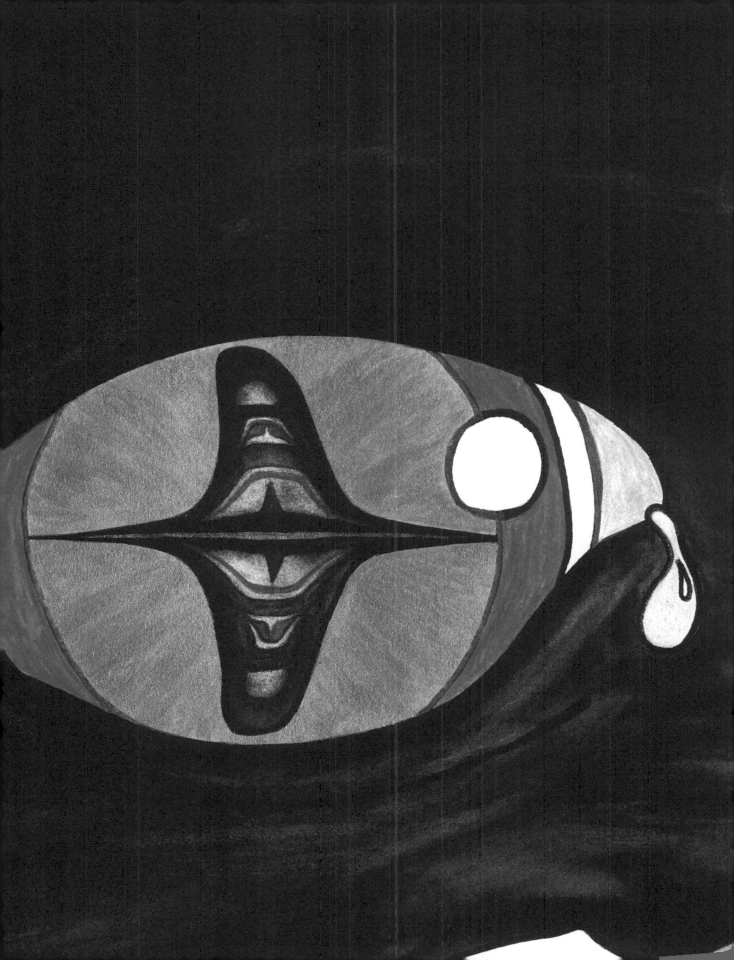

For you see, she was not lost after all; she had just joined her loved ones of the sea. And even though she had left her human life behind, Kún Jáadaas knew she and the Haida people would one day reunite. Although they lived in different worlds, they would always be close to help, comfort, and love each other. After all, family is family. Together, the people and the whales felt the ever so quiet wonder that told them the world is truly magic!

ACKNOWLEDGMENTS

I would like to give thanks to all who helped me in completing this book. First, I want to thank our Creator for everything. To my children: Sorrel, Seri, and Shea, to whom I read my story over and over again until I got it right. Thank you for your patience and input. To my parents and family for believing in me. To Sealaska Heritage Institute for helping to fund production of my book and publishing it. To Potlatch Fund and Evergreen Longhouse for awarding me grant money to provide the tools and supplies needed. To my cousin, Ben Young, who worked with the elders in our village to translate my words into our Haida language. To my Haida elders Uncle Miijuu (Claude Morrison) and Auntie Viola Burgess for translating. To our Haida linguist Jordan Lachler for the correct spelling. Finally, to all my students and their parents for their support and encouragement. Haw'aa/Thank you!

ABOUT THE AUTHOR

Sondra comes from the Double Fin Killer Whale Crest, Brown Bear House, and Raven Clan. Her maternal grandparents are Haida from Southeast Alaska. Through them, she has learned to keep their culture alive through music, hearing them speak Kaigani Xaadaas (Alaskan Haida—an almost extinct language), continuing to eat traditional foods, honoring their ancient art form, often visiting their tribal village (Hydaburg), and staying close to their Northwest Coast Native family and community in Seattle where she resides.

IMAGE OF SONDRA CREATED BY STEPHANIE STEVENS.

It is very important for Sondra to help preserve her culture and she does this in many ways:

- Sondrasimone.com is her contemporary Native art business where she creates a variety of custom Haida designs.

- Sondra and her family make traditional regalia to wear in

performances for their dance group The Haida Heritage Foundation, for which she is current drum and dance leader.

- She writes and illustrates children's picture books and art instruction books based on her culture.

- To help keep her language alive, she writes and sings songs which have been translated into Haida.

In her daily life, Sondra is a full time educator and enjoys singing gospel music.

Creating this book has been a long journey and has brought her so much happiness and healing. She hopes you enjoy reading it as much as she has enjoyed making it.

CPSIA information can be obtained
at www.ICGtesting.com
Printed in the USA
LVHW07n0155140518
577077LV00005B/31/P